MÀMÁ, IT'S A GIRL

MÀMÁ, IT'S A GIRL

STELLA DAMASUS

To request permissions, contact the publisher at
adivanetworks@gmail.com

Title: MÀMÁ, IT'S A GIRL / Author: Stella Damasus
ISBN 979-8-9859311-0-5 (Paperback)
ISBN 979-8-9859311-1-2 (Hardcover)
ISBN 979-8-9859311-2-9 (Audiobook)
ISBN 979-8-9859311-3-6 (EBook)
Library of Congress Control Number: 2023931924

The characters and events in this book are fictitious. Any
similarity to real persons, living or dead, is coincidental and
not intended by the author.

Editing by Precious Mogoli & ADIVA Networks
Front cover Art (Illustration) by Ejiro Lane
Book design by Ruméh Ejoor
Author's Photography IzzyBelle Images

Printed and bound in the United States of America
First printing March 2023
Published by ADIVA Networks
9900 Westpark Dr STE 328
Houston, Texas, 77063

First Edition

Visit www.stelladamasus.com/author

◀◀◀☙———APPRECIATION———☙▶▶▶

I want to thank those who supported and encouraged me to keep writing, even though I was afraid no one would want to read my book: my late father, Chief S.K.C. Damasus; my late mother, Chief Mrs. M.T. Damasus; my siblings, Shirley, Kate, Sandra, Sylvia, and their families. My Mentor, Qodesh Ejoor; who has taught me and prayed for me. Segun Lawal, my Uncle Daddy, who kept pushing and guiding me. Alex Okoroji, you gave me the courage to go into publishing.

The Ejoor family, who have become my own family, thank you for your constant words of encouragement and prayer. Ruméh Ejoor, the one I call my right hand. I will never have enough words to express my gratitude for the love, support, listening ear, creativity, and loyalty. You are more than a creative director; you are family. Thank you.

My daughters Isabel and Angelica, thank you for always putting a smile on my face. For supporting me through this process. I could not have asked for better children. This book is one of the fruits of your prayers and encouragement, and it is my prayer that you will do bigger, better, and greater things than your parents.

Jaiyejeje Aboderin, you will always be in my heart.

I thank my Lord in heaven, who created me in His own image and made me the woman I am.

To all my friends, I love you.

◄◄◄◦── ABOUT THE ARTWORK ──◦►►►

*This artwork tells the story of Teno, a female child from
Kaminwanaga. It begins with the outline of her head as a young girl.
The speech bubble represents her thoughts, which she isn't allowed to
voice. It ends with her image as a woman with a speech bubble on the
outside. This depicts her ability to speak freely. Between both stages of
her life, you can see the different situations that make her the woman
she has become.*
Such as the tears, which represent pain;
the sickle, which means death;
the ocean, which depicts her traveling abroad,
a cross representing her religion;
*The flower blossoming represents becoming a woman and the
villagers celebrating, which depicts her impact on the people of
Kaminwanaga.*

Art by Ejiro Lane

◄◄◄⊙━━ REVIEW ━━⊙►►►

This story is so real, and everyone who reads it would quickly identify with the characters. How the craving for money can push a father to label his daughter just because she seeks a better life for herself but accepts and allows his son to carry on irresponsibly. Stella Damasus has always been vocal about ending child marriage in Nigeria, especially in Africa. Many people who know she is an advocate for the girl child will understand why 'Màmá, it's a girl' is not just a work of fiction but a heart-cry to all.

- Sandra Damasus Chime -Age, CEO, Design S3

MÀMÁ, IT'S A GIRL is a gripping tale of a nameless girl who rose from the ashes of abject dehumanization of the girl child to the peak of success. It is a very emotional read that will definitely force tears down your cheeks. The message in this beautiful piece can never be lost on anyone who loves to see the promotion of pristine humanity for both the female and male genders. MÀMÁ, IT'S A GIRL is a reminder that no matter how long darkness has ruled, light will completely decimate it; love always trumps hatred, and resilience definitely crushes hitherto entrenched mountains of impossibilities. MÀMÁ, IT'S A GIRL, after all, is not in any way less joyful news to MÀMÁ, IT'S A BOY!

- Pastor Jerry Eze, convener of the New Season Prophetic Prayers (NSPPD) and Lead Pastor of Streams of Joy International.

This is a must read book. The lead character represents so many girls born in Africa who have had to experience and endure the violation of their rights. She tells the story of her life from birth and takes us on a journey; through the lives of other girls like her and even worse. This book will take you on an emotional and psychological journey. It will also show you how one person can make a significant impact on society and change the current narrative for the better.

- Abubakar Tafawa-Balewa, Editor In Chief at MODE MEN MAGAZINE

REVIEW

Màmá, It's A Girl is a gut-wrenching story of a character who exemplifies what it looks like to be female in Africa - the marginalisation, the stereotyping, the frustrations, dangers and struggles that women truly experience and have to endure from birth. This book shows the possibilities that can emerge when we empower women and support them with love and opportunities to thrive. A creatively written fiction story that is worth reading.

- Alex Okoroji, Actress and Founder & President of The BRAG Media Group

Through this powerful story of a young girl born in a village in Africa, Stella provides a window into the harsh reality and brutal discrimination millions face just because of being born a girl. Through simple yet soulful writing, Stella conveys how change is possible when a woman, in the face of adversity, dares to dream of a better future for herself, her family and her community. This journey – overcoming discrimination through courage and resilience - is one we at Women for Women International see in the hundreds of thousands of women we serve in conflict-affected regions across the world. Màmá, It's A Girl is a heartwarming and poignant story illuminating the ripple effect of women coming together in solidarity and realizing our power.

- Laurie Adams, CEO, Women for Women International

‹‹‹◦—— FOREWORD ——◦›››

Mission Accomplished!

That was my dominant thought when in one day, I read through this fascinating book. I just could not put it down.

Written in a simple easy-to-read style, this book will stir your soul, whip up your sentiments and inspire a greater understanding of the African woman. Hopefully, it will also propel you to some form of action, no matter how small.

The author's journey through heartbreak, disappointment, rejection, and recovery positioned her to deliver this story with much empathy.

It has been a great privilege to be one of her mentors, watch her blossom again and begin to exploit her many talents. She is a shiny example of the countless gifts and strong resilience that lies in the bosom of the African woman.

It is a new dawn. A time to push back the oppressive traditions against women, not only for the present generation but also for the next generation of girls they will nurture.

I strongly recommend this book to those who have a sincere passion for Africa and the rights of women worldwide.

- Qodesh Ejoor

◄◄◄○── INTRODUCTION ──○►►►

When I toyed with the idea of writing a book and sharing my thoughts with the world, it was supposed to be a fun, playful storybook. That would have been much easier for me to write. But, seeing some of the things that so many women around me had experienced, I decided it was best to tell this story.

Being born a female in Africa is more challenging than it might be in other parts of the world. As an African woman, I've seen and spoken with women who have been through significant challenges. From birth, their challenges were unique simply because they were born and raised in Africa. I have merged some of these stories through the life, and the eyes, of a female character.

I believe this book will propel you to act or be more aware of the plight of the African girl, and I hope you will enjoy this book as a story with a mission.

- Stella Damasus

Contents

CHAPTER ONE

A Girl Is Born

SHE TWISTED AND TURNED IN HER BED, clenching her teeth to avoid screaming her lungs off. The pain was excruciating. Tears rolled down her cheeks as she held tightly to her husband's arm. Denkamali was in so much pain, she thought her end was near.

She was tall, light-skinned, and gorgeous. Deep dimples on both cheeks. She kept her hair natural. It was very thick, black, and long. Fondly called Denka, she was the dream woman of every man's fantasy, at least every man in the beautiful African village of KAMINWANAGA. Every man wanted her but, her heart was set solely on one man, Bebami.

Beba was not as tall as Denka but was handsome, rugged, and had the boldness of a lion. He had a piercing look and dark skin further bronzed by the sun due to years of laboring and working outdoors. He was not wealthy, but he was hard-working, and Denka loved how his sweat made him glow in the sun after a hard day's work; she found it attractive; she felt safe in his arms. In Beba, she found a provider, a soul mate, and a protector.

Today, however, even the man in her life, her protector, her husband, could not take away the labor pain she was feeling.

She did not expect the pain to be that much but, she had to be strong. Denka could not afford to cry too loudly so that her neighbors would not have cause to laugh and call her weak. Bebami tried to calm her down, but his efforts yielded little results.

"I can't take this anymore!" Denka grunted out to Bebami, "get the midwife now, Beba!"

She was ready to have the baby, so Beba ran out to get the village midwife, an elderly woman in her 70s. She had been a midwife for four decades and was responsible for the birth of 90% of the children in Kaminwanaga. Beba returned with the woman and her two assistants and had to wait outside because it was taboo for a man to be in the same room with his wife during delivery. As he waited expectantly and paced anxiously, some neighbors joined him and offered words of comfort and encouragement.

Inside, the midwife screamed at Denkamali, instructing her to stay strong and push the baby out.

"I'm trying!" Denka yelled back in pain, "I'm trying."

"You are just shouting; you are not pushing. Push! Push!" the midwife yelled back, and with one final scream, "Aaaaaarrrgghhhhh!" Denka pushed with every ounce of energy she could summon from within and the world beyond.

"Waaaahhhh!!!". The baby came out kicking and screaming. Clearly, this young one couldn't wait to breathe in some fresh air and be liberated from the womb of the mother. The baby's voice sounded like little chimes being rattled violently, though, by a strong wind. But what was going on?

The midwife brought out a very sharp local knife, grabbed the umbilical cord, and started to cut. Pause for a moment so you can imagine the picture I am painting here. In her late 70s, this midwife was very dark-skinned and had yellow teeth, most of which were missing. She had wrinkled and very shaky hands, maybe because of age or an illness. She held the knife that looked like it had been decades since water, soap, or any sort of sterilizing material touched it. How could this be healthy? How could this be sanitary? The midwife smiled as she wiped the baby clean.

"Such a beauty," she said.

Denka asked, "Please YaYa, what did I have?" The midwife did not respond but handed her the baby and said sternly, "My work here is done."

As YaYa left the room, the smiling baby looked up to see its mother's face.

"My goodness, this must be the most beautiful human in the world," the baby must have thought to itself. Rather than smile back, Denka broke into tears. Why would a mother cry at the sight of her new baby?

"God, why me?" she asked amidst tears, "why me?"

Even the baby looked stunned. Thoughts in the baby's head must have been, "Is this how they celebrate in the real world? Did I do something wrong?"

Meanwhile, outside the house, there was another round of drama unfolding. As the midwife emerged with her assistants, Bebami's mother, simply called Ma-Beba, rushed into the compound and moved quickly to her side. She heard the baby's cry from inside the house and embraced her son as a proud grandmother would. Ma-Beba looked at YaYa happily and asked for the gender of the baby; she simply told her to go in and find out. Ma-Beba grabbed Beba by the arm, looked him straight in the eyes, and said, "I hope for your sake it's a boy."

Fearfully, Beba asked his mother to go in and find out.

Ma-Beba walked into the room to see Denka in tears with her back turned to the baby crying on the bed. Denka knew the drill and did not have to wait for the inevitable question; slowly, she looked up and said,

"MÀMÁ, IT'S A GIRL!"

Ma-Beba screamed and ran outside. She looked at Bebami, hissed, and then yelled, "Abomination!" as she angrily stormed out of the compound. Bebami was petrified. It felt like a boulder smashed his gut. How could this be? Not again, not another girl. No, not another girl. He buried his face in his hands as he leaned against the wall like a man who just had his life sucked right out of him.

By the way, I was that little baby girl, and this is my story.

***

I come from a very traditional community where Western education and the western way of life for girls are unfamiliar to us. We believe in our culture, local gods, and history passed down from one generation to the next. So let me formally welcome you to my hometown, known as Kaminwanaga. That is a funny name, right? Do not worry; there are more to come.

Kaminwanaga is a beautiful place with lots of trees, rivers, lovely huts, and good vegetation. Growing up, we all ate food from our farms and drank water from our streams. The women covered their bodies with nice Aga clothes and had beautiful tattoos on their arms to show which family they come from. The sunlight was very friendly, and when it rained, we blessed the gods for showering their blessing on our crops. The children would always come out to play, and dance in the rain with absolutely no cares in the world.

Now that you know where I come from, let me explain why my parents and Ma-Beba were unhappy at my birth.

The fate of the girl-child in Kaminwanaga is not a very pleasant one. According to our history, all families throw their second female child in the Wailing River because they see her as waste and a liability. So, if a family has the first female, she is kept to take over the chores from her mother, and then from the age of nine, she can be sold off into marriage. To my people, there was no need for another female child; only boys were needed. I was only spared because my sister was sold off way before I was born, and my parents needed help with the chores; being born late saved me.

Beba was sad, as he knew he would be laughed at because he did not have a boy who would have continued with the family name after the first girl. The girl child would only eat his food and not amount to anything other than being a commodity to be sold off for almost nothing to an interested buyer. From Denka's point of view, she would be seen as an evil woman who did not want her husband to be prosperous and respected. She would also be seen as worse than barren, for in Kaminwanaga, it is better not to have children at all than to have two girls. Only the love of her husband would keep her from being thrown out.

Did you just ask if my people believe that children

come from women, and the gender of the child is determined by the woman? Then the answer is YES! Ma-Beba was unhappy that her son could not share in the feasts from the festival nor take up any position in the village council. So, you see, no matter how you look at it, I am an abomination in the land of Kaminwanaga.

***

I was three years old when my mother gave birth to a boy; this made everyone happy, far from what happened when I was born. There was a celebration with people coming to congratulate my father on finally becoming worthy of being called a man in the eyes of the Village Council. It became clear to me that the birth of a boy calls for celebration, but the birth of a girl is an abomination. As time passed, I realized that MEBO (short for MEBONDIBA), my brother, could do no wrong, but I was scolded and beaten at the slightest provocation. Whenever Mebo did something wrong, especially to me, he would scream and act like he was dying even before I did anything to him. My mother would then run out and say, "Why are you doing this? And whenever I tried to explain, she would yell, "Shut up! Don't you know you should be treating him with respect? Don't forget he is a boy, soon to be a MAN!"

Mebo got whatever he wanted, especially the things I could not get, just because he was a boy. I remember the day I tried to take an extra piece of yam; after Mebo had taken two additional pieces, my father screamed at me and said that his financial problems started the day I was born.

Anyway, I had heard worse things from him already, so it was no longer a big deal.

The time came for me to go to school, and my parents kept telling me that Western education was a waste of time. At this time, I was almost ten years old, and Mebo was seven. I considered myself lucky because there was no interested buyer other than the old man who came to ask for my hand in marriage. I was so rude to him when he came to our home; I even told him he would die if he took me to his house as his wife. Of course, my father almost killed me for saying that to him.

Don't get me wrong, I was a charming girl, but after word spread in my village about how rude and stubborn I was, no one wanted me as a wife. I was actually polite but had to behave like that in public just to create an impression in the minds of the silly old men who were looking for little girls to marry. I was happy because I got to stay in my home with my family, and even though it made my father despise me more, I didn't mind.

One day I found my father dressing Mebo up and telling him to go to school and become successful so he could take care of the family. Shocked, I ran inside crying; it hurt so much, it was as if I had been stabbed in the heart. Denka came to me and asked why I was crying, and I reminded her that they said it was a waste of time to learn how to read and write, but Mebo was being sent to school. I asked my mother what I had done to deserve this. She looked at me square in the eyes and said, "YOU ARE A GIRL!"

CHAPTER TWO

The Girl Is Now A Woman

MY FRIENDS AND I WOULD PLAY under the cherry tree; I am not sure about the proper name, but the local name is ZáZá. Every evening after farm work and just before dinner, we would gather to tell stories, dance, and sing our traditional folk songs. At that time, I was almost 11 years old. For about five days, I noticed that I did not see one of my best friends, TANDORALI. I called her TANDO, and she loved it, but her family always called her Tandorali.

This got me worried, so I decided to go to her house where I saw her father, who was almost 50 years old. Apart from not liking that I did not add the RALI to Tando, he acted very strangely when I asked after her. Anyway, he told me she had traveled and wouldn't be back for a long time. Being inquisitive, I asked when she left and why she didn't tell any of her friends. This probably aggravated him, and so he asked me to leave his house and never come back. I knew something was wrong, but I didn't know what it was.

As I was walking home, I saw BANTAKIBA, one of my friends, Tando's neighbor. She asked me where I was coming from, and I told her what had happened at Tando's house. Banta expressed her worries over Tando's disappearance. All she remembered was people she had never seen before gathered at Tando's home for a party. At first, BANTA thought nothing of it until she saw Tando crying with a bag on her head and was being led out of the compound by some elderly women. Bantakiba said she walked by the side of the house and saw Tando's mother crying too; after that party, she never saw Tando again.

What could this mean?

How can a party make people cry?

Where did they take Tando?

Will she ever return? Where is Tando?

These were all questions in my head with no one to answer them, because as a girl, I was not allowed to ask such questions.

***

A year had passed, and I was finally allowed to go to

the market on my own. After buying all I was asked to buy, I carried my bag of goods and as I turned around, standing behind me was my dear friend Tando!

I hugged her and screamed, but she quickly covered my mouth and told me not to draw any attention. I stepped back, looked at her, and saw that she was not really the same Tando I knew; she was a shadow of herself. I asked why she looked the way she did, skinny, dirty, and dressed like an old woman. She shook her head sadly, looked at me, and replied, "That's because I am a woman."

At first, it sounded funny to me, so I laughed because she was only a year older than I was, but when I looked into her eyes, I knew it was time to talk. I pulled her to a private corner by the side of the bush path and begged my friend to talk.

Tando broke down uncontrollably, and it made my heart sink. I had to calm her down so she could tell me the whole story. Knowing what I now know of that story, I wish I had never asked.

Tando asked me, "Do you remember one day when

I came to our meeting place but had to leave immediately, and it upset you?"

I remembered the day she was talking about; I was upset because I had avoided a chore at home to hang out with my friend, but she ditched me. I got back home to some scolding from my parents. How could I forget the day?

Tando continued, "I left because the pain was too much for me to bear, so I had to go home and lie down."

"What pain?" I asked.

"The pain of womanhood," she replied.

With tears in her eyes and pain in her heart, she told me this horrible story:

"One day, I came home from the farm, and my father told me I would be going somewhere with my aunt. As I went in to change, my aunt followed me and gave me a white wrapper, saying it was more appropriate for where we were going. As we got to the village square, some girls, who were crying, were led by scary-looking elderly women. These girls were all dressed like me. As I turned to ask my aunty what we were doing there, she grabbed my arm and handed me over to one of the elderly women. We stopped moving, and they dragged one of the girls to the floor, one woman holding her hands and another holding her legs. She continued crying as the oldest woman brought out a wicked-looking blade from a calabash. The girl struggled and screamed. The woman slapped her and asked another woman to put a piece of cloth in her mouth. The old woman then lowered the blade to her private area and cut her seed (clitoris)."

I screamed and asked her why they did that. Tando looked at me with tear-soaked eyes and said, "I asked the old woman why they would do that to me, and she simply said it was because I was becoming a woman. According to tradition, that was my transition process into womanhood."

I was speechless as she continued, "This was all to prepare me as payment for the debt my father could not settle. I was given away to a man old enough to be my grandfather. I am not only a woman now; I am a wife."

CHAPTER THREE

Ticket To Freedom

IT WAS A HOT DAY TODAY at the farm, and I was so exhausted. The giant palm tree was calling my name. It was inviting me to sit under its excellent shade, calling me to leave the heat of the blazing sun that left sweat cascading down my face and …blah, blah, blah. Okay, that's just me trying to sound poetic and very intelligent; if it didn't work, just ignore that and continue with the story.

As I sat under the tree, Banta, who was also very tired, walked up to me as she had also succumbed to the invitation of the tree's shade. That was when she told me of the beautiful, white, long-nosed woman with hair so long and soft it moved in the wind; she had tiny lips and skin like the morning sun. She said her clothes were so sophisticated and bright that they could light up a room. When she spoke, it seemed like the words came out of her nose. People just loved to listen to her even if they didn't really understand what she was saying. It was surprising to me because I was usually the first amongst all my friends to get information like this.

You see, I didn't tell you before how brilliant I am if I may say so myself. It was effortless for me to understand, memorize, imitate, and study things that were difficult for my peers.

On the other hand, my brother, Mebo, who was chosen to get an education, was not the sharpest tool in the shed. He struggled to retain information and was always frustrated with schoolwork.

Banta said this white lady was a missionary who served a strange god. She was sent from the white man's land as one of the people to bring education to African girls. The school was free, and the girls would learn to read and write. My heart started beating fast as I immediately remembered my father always saying Mebo must succeed in school. He believed that learning to read and write was the Road to Freedom. He would tell Mebo how the ability to read and write was his ticket to the city, and the city is the Land of Freedom. I knew right away that I did not want to end up like Tando.

I wanted the freedom to live the life I always dreamt

about, the life we heard of in the stories about the city from those fortunate enough to go there. They brought magazines sometimes, and though we could not read them, we loved the pictures we saw, especially of the women in the city. My mind was made up, Banta had to take me there, but we couldn't tell anyone. I was going to get my ticket to freedom!

***

Banta and I knew we had to cut our time on the farm in half. We snuck out and ran as fast as we could to get to the white morning sun, sorry, White Woman. When we got there, we saw a few other girls from the village and two of our friends. Finally, I could hardly wait to see her.

As we all sat down on the long benches in the spacious room, a door opened, and there she was. She was so beautiful I could have sworn we were just visited by an angel. When she spoke, I could not hear anything else but her voice. Not even the sound of birds, not the sound of the leaves rustling in response to the command of the afternoon breeze; everything else was utterly isolated and eliminated. I could only hear the words coming out of her mouth, words I could not understand.

I felt like I was dining with the gods. She smiled and started trying to break down her words. A young black lady walked in, gave her a hug, and then shocked us by speaking in our language.

She said she was once like us but was lucky to run to the city where she learned to read and write. Her place of learning was owned by a missionary who liked her and sent her to America to continue her studies in Language and Art. After that, she started teaching in her Church, which was where she met MISS THERESA. That was the name of the white woman, and her own name was MARY. So, Miss Theresa would teach, and Mary would translate.

Before we left that day, Miss Theresa looked at me with those angelic eyes and asked, "What is your name?" Mary helped to interpret, and I responded excitedly.

"My name is TENONDIBA, but I like it when people call me TENO."

As Miss Theresa smiled back and rubbed her soft hands on the side of my face, I melted like shea butter beside firewood. I was ready to learn; I was ready to be free.

CHAPTER FOUR

My Journey Begins

I HAVE BEEN SO BUSY with school and the other chores I have to do. Guess what? I can read and write, at least to a certain degree. Oh please! Don't give me that tiny smirk; celebrate with me. Roll out the drums and tambourines. Raise your voices and shout with joy to the mountaintops because you don't understand what it means for someone like me to read and write. In your society today, it is normal for children to grow up learning to read and write. However, in Kaminwanaga, I learned to read in the shadows, hiding away from the prying eyes of tradition. A tradition that would not give me access to education, access to my ticket to freedom.

Anyway, Miss Theresa liked me very much, and our relationship was becoming more like that of a mother and daughter. One day, I asked her why she treated me as special, and she said I was the most promising girl in her school. She often wondered why I was extremely determined and eager to learn faster than others were.

I had to tell her my story, and when I got to Tando's part, tears rolled freely down her face. I believe, at that moment, she finally understood the meaning of what she was doing, the hope we were given, and the lives she was saving. It seemed like my story, my words, were a confirmation of her purpose here on earth.

Miss Theresa held my hand and promised that she would give me extra classes and make sure I could read and write correctly. She also said that I should become a journalist because of my inquisitive nature, the quest for knowledge, and the search for the truth.

On a particular day, I was the only one in school because Miss Theresa kept her promise to give me extra classes. She wanted to make sure I had my ticket to freedom. Suddenly, the door burst open, and Miss Mary ran in. She asked Miss Theresa to come with her to see something that couldn't be explained verbally. Miss Theresa was worried and asked if I could wait for her, but being the curious little girl I was, going with her was what my heart wanted; I followed my heart. We walked so fast that I thought people from America had wheels embedded in their feet. The sun was high up in the sky, and the heat seemed to penetrate my scalp. How could this white woman still be fully functional and this fast in this heat?

It was very far into the woods, but we finally got in front of an abandoned building. The smell coming from the place was so bad that Miss Theresa started coughing and vomiting. She held her nose and continued until Miss Mary opened the door; what we saw changed our lives forever.

Young girls, not more than 13 years old, were lying on the floor, with some even at the point of death. They had uncontrollable leakages; they could not hold or control their urine. Miss Mary explained that these girls had been dropped and left here by their husbands to rot away and die far from their homes. They were all mothers who had to go through unsafe childbirths. Miss Theresa cried and asked what they could do to help. Miss Mary suggested they could do a report and send it to the Church in America.

As we turned around to leave, I heard a frail voice calling out, "Teno! Teno! It's me!"

I turned around with my heart pounding. Oh no!

"Tando!" There she was, my dear friend who was married off by her parents as payment for her father's debt. There she lay in the filth, condemned to death because of her parents' actions; my heart sank.

A very heartbroken Miss Theresa wrote a long letter to the Church that sent her to Kaminwanaga. She told them of the discovery we made in the woods and asked them to help. She cried as she wrote, and it broke my heart to see my beautiful and happy Miss Theresa cry so much. How did one who barely knew these girls have so much love and compassion in her heart for them?

***

After a few months of meeting with Miss Theresa for my extra classes, I noticed that she had become a bit withdrawn. Her smile was fading quickly, and it worried me. When I asked Miss Mary to tell me why she was in that mood, she said they had received a reply to the letter. The Church said it could help with money and food for the people but could not authorize or support moving the girls from the building as requested. It did not want to interfere or meddle in traditional and customary rites or beliefs, as it was not in its place to go against tradition. Kaminwanaga had already given permission to set up a place for a missionary school. They did not want to strain that relationship. Miss Theresa was advised to send the girls food if she wanted to, but that was as far as she could go.

One of the saddest days in my life was when I told Miss Theresa of my decision to leave for the city. We both cried because we had built a strong bond that I had never had with anyone else. She encouraged me to take my freedom and go to the city. She knew I would be successful and help my community, especially the young girls who would otherwise face the same fate as Tando.

I got home and broke the news of my moving to the city. My father, who was not feeling too well, said to me, "I always knew you were a mistake, a prostitute who would bring us shame and disgrace. You should have ended up in the Wailing River like others. You know that the girls in the city are all prostitutes, yet it is attractive to you."

At that point, I had become so immune to his hurtful words, so I just stared at him, dead-eyed and speechless. Mother was confused and wondered where I summoned the courage to speak like that and make such a decision. Mebo walked in smiling after selling only five jars of Moonshine, which we call Ogogoro in Africa. As he approached me, I figured he probably drank more jars than he sold. Mebo smelled as if he just fell out of a barrel filled with Ogogoro.

Oh! Forgive me. I forgot to tell you that Mebo dropped out of school some time ago and started selling Ogogoro. A total disappointment, but as usual, I was called a witch, one who destroyed his future out of envy.

Before anyone woke up the following day, I was already at the motor park (bus station) to find transportation to the city. As I got into the truck and we started moving, my village got further and further away.

This was the start of my journey to freedom; it was the happiest day of my life.

CHAPTER FIVE

Bright Lights

THE CITY WAS DIFFERENT from what I had heard. Everything was high-speed! There were lights in the streets and tall buildings trying to get to the sky; women dressed like Miss Theresa and Miss Mary, but some were dressed in a way that was not appropriate for a woman. All of a sudden, I felt so small and insignificant in this big place. Don't get me wrong, I was very excited and hoped for the best. Since I didn't know anyone there, I decided to walk around for a while.

By sunset, I noticed people were trooping in and out of a store at the end of the street. I walked in and asked for the owner, who then came out and asked what I wanted. I told her about my situation and how I got to the city, but she walked me out and asked me never to return. "Is this how people in the city are?" I wondered.

As I walked out, I saw a long bench by the building and sat on it; I was so tired that I dozed off. By the time I opened my eyes, it was a new day. The shop owner, who obviously saw me asleep on the bench on her way home the night before, asked me to come inside the shop. That was how I got my first job as a shop attendant; my salary was shelter and food. The storeowner began to like me, and before I knew it, she got me nice clothes and took me to get my first perm.

I knew I had arrived; I was a city girl at last and had found a place to start chasing my dream of becoming a journalist. I knew I had to start from the bottom up, and I was ready for my humble beginning. I had hoped for a life in the city where I could become anything. This was it.

My room was behind Madam's house, and on this fateful night, as I was praying (yes, Miss Theresa taught me about Jesus and God, and The Lord's Prayer too). My doorknob started turning. I thought it was Madam, but it was her husband. I quickly sat up on my bed and asked if I could do something for him; he smiled and sat on my bed.

"Teno, do you know you are a very beautiful girl?" he asked as he reached out to touch my lap. I quickly covered it with my small blanket and moved out of his reach.

"Ah! Please, sir. It's not good for you to touch me like

that, sir," I pleaded. "If madam comes in here right now, she will kill me."

His eyes were cold and dead as they pierced my soul. My words fell on deaf ears as his eyes undressed me even to my bones. At that point, I knew that there was nothing I could say to stop him, so I started yelling for help, but no one heard me, no one came.

He grabbed me and became very violent. He tore my clothes and forced himself on me. It was the worst thing that had ever happened to me. I screamed. I cried. My tears were not just because of what was happening to me, but because I finally felt the real pain Tando must have felt when she was given away.

He raped me violently.

That was it!

My virginity was gone! Was that really it?

The next day, I was too sore to even leave my bed, let alone go to work. Madam had waited for me for a while, and when I didn't show up, she stormed into my room. I was crying in bed with blood on my sheets. At first, she asked if I was on my period, and I said no. She kept asking till she got impatient, so I told her the truth, and all hell broke loose. You cannot begin to imagine how a story like this was flipped around to make me the ungrateful prostitute who came to seduce her employer's husband. I didn't realize that even in the city, girls were still treated as second-class citizens. Do I need to tell you on whose side Madam was? What could I have done? Maybe I should have said I was on my period. But that meant Madam's husband would have had the opportunity to do it repeatedly.

NO!

I did the right thing and suffered the consequences.

It was better than proving my father right.

No Work. No Food. No Shelter. Back to square one.

As I walked along the city's busy streets, I saw an arrow pointing to the left. On top of the needle was a sign that read, 'CHURCH OF BIG DREAMS.' Beside the signboard was the picture of the Pastor and his wife, whom I recognized because I had seen him on television during my time working at the store. Since I had no other choice, I decided to walk to the Church and see if I could get a roof over my head.

I got there and was referred to a nice-looking lady who listened to my story. When I was done talking, she took me to one of the small classrooms and said I could sleep there, but I had to get up and clean it before 5 a.m.

Miss Theresa taught me that no matter what my situation was, as long as I could run into the house of God, I would be safe. True to her words, they took care of me and kept me busy.

I finally met the Pastor after he heard how intelligent I was and what I was doing to help manage the church building. That day he gave me an envelope and said he was blessing me. Too afraid to look inside, I didn't open it till I got back to the small classroom that had been given to me as my room.

As I finished my prayers, I dared to open the envelope and believe me, I had never seen that kind of money in my entire life. Hurriedly, I put aside my tithe to be paid the following Sunday. Miss Theresa had taught me about that, and this Pastor had talked about it on one of his television broadcasts I saw a while back. It was the right thing to do. A few days later, as I got to my room, I saw a parcel with a note inside that read,

"The more diligent you are, the more blessings you will

receive."

I opened the big box and found double the amount the Pastor had given me previously. Also in the box were some clothes and jewelry.

After a while, I noticed that all the people I worked with started acting funny towards me. They ended conversations as soon as I walked into a room or would simply walk past me without responding to my greetings. It was weird and uncomfortable. I tried to find out why but no one wanted to speak to me; they all gave me the cold shoulder. I got scared and went to see the Pastor, who was like a father to me by then.

He said, "Sometimes when God separates you to bless you, even your family will be jealous." The Pastor continued and said, "Look at Joseph in the Bible. When he dreamt about his greatness, it became obvious that he was more special than his brothers. They grew jealous and sold him into slavery. You have been more faithful, diligent, and committed than anybody else here. That is why you are receiving divine favor and blessings. If Joseph's blood brothers could be jealous of him, why shouldn't people around you here be jealous of you?"

His words brought me comfort and stirred up more confidence in my spirit. He asked me to go to my room because there was something I had to see. I got to my door and found all my belongings on the floor with a note that read,

"Get the keys to your new apartment at the security post."

It was like a dream; Miss Theresa's God was so awesome! I couldn't even contain myself. I took my keys, and the Church's bus driver drove me to a more beautiful house than my former Madam's main house. If it was a dream, I didn't want to wake up. I knelt down and thanked God with tears of joy.

***

Unfortunately, the hostility and hatred towards me grew in the Church, which brought a lot of drama. I was constantly getting insulted and verbally attacked by church staff and some members for no real reason. As time went by, things got out of hand, and I could not bear it anymore. I went back to my father in the Lord, my Pastor, and what he said had the effect of being shot in the head with the bullet traveling slowly through my brain.

"Do not mind them, my love; they are all jealous because they know how I feel about you," he said.

I was confused and needed him to clarify.

"They know I am in love with you, and you are special to me; they do that all the time."

"All the time? So, this happens regularly?" I asked.

He laughed as he brought two glasses and a bottle out of which he poured a drink with about 20% alcohol (believing that I saw the label correctly). He asked me to drink with him; horrified, I asked why.

He said, "I want you to relax so you can dance for me, sweetheart."

"God forbid! What has come over you, Pastor? Why are you doing this?"

He got angry and yelled, "Who would you rather give yourself to? A random guy who cannot offer you much or one with a special anointing and grace that will cover you and make all your sins disappear?"

At this point, there was nothing left to say other than, "I

am leaving; thank you for all your help."

"No problem," he blurted out, "but you cannot take anything I bought for you, and you cannot stay in that house. If you go, don't ever return!"

Thank God I had saved some money; I carried the same bag I had brought from the village and left. Did I hear you say back to the streets again? Wrong. I had some money, so I would be fine, or so I thought.

After staying in a small hotel for three weeks, I ran out of money; I was shocked! I didn't even spend anything on myself. Is this how expensive the city is? Back in Kaminwanaga, my money would have bought me a piece of land, built a house, and gotten me a chieftaincy title.

Okay, now you can say it - BACK TO SQUARE ONE!

CHAPTER SIX

A Ray Of Hope

WOW! THIS WAS NOT WHAT I EXPECTED,
but I guess my head was in the clouds, and I was too naive to
understand what life was about outside my village. When I was
with my Madam, she bought me a cheap cell phone, and when
I was kicked out, she was so angry she forgot to take it back; I
promptly changed the SIM card.

I remembered NEMA, one of the girls I met while at the
shop; she was one of my favorite customers who was so nice
and told me to call her if I ever needed to talk to a friend.

I guessed that time had come, so I called her, and we
met at her house, which was comfortable and neatly furnished.
It was beautiful with nice colors. It felt like home. As I sat
down to talk with Nema, I couldn't stop wondering. I asked
myself how many years of education she went through to get a
job that made it possible for her to afford such a place.

After telling her everything, she let me stay with her.
She went to work only at night, so I concluded, "She must be a

nurse!" I was so impressed by how much she was making as a nurse that I began to wonder if I still wanted to be a journalist.

After about six months of looking for work with no luck, I got so depressed. Then one evening, Nema came to my room and said I had to start paying half the rent and contributing money for food. She even gave me a deadline to meet or risk being kicked out. I explained my unsuccessful job search, and she said I could join her line of work. My confusion was instant, so I said, "Nema, do you know how long it will take me to attend school and get trained to be a nurse?"

"Seriously, Teno, after six months, you still think I'm a nurse?" she asked, almost feeling sorry for me.

Slowly, she eased herself into the couch beside me and explained what her occupation was. Well, let's just say she was not a nurse, a doctor, or a police officer; the long coat she wore at night was to cover her skimpy clothes. Joining Nema in her work would fulfill my father's statement about what I would become in the city. I couldn't bear the thought of that; I could never do that.

The deadline came, and I was sent out. This time I was

totally wiped out, sad, alone, afraid, depressed, angry, and desperate. After roaming the treacherous streets of the city and sleeping in abandoned commercial buses for a few nights, I came across a sign that read HIRING. I got in there, passed my interview, which really didn't seem like an interview, and started working for a printing press.

I had to wear an ugly uniform and work with big printing machines, so I always had black ink all over my face and clothes. It was a hard job, but I was committed to being the best I could be. I learned how the machines worked, I asked many questions. In no time, I was entrusted with operating specific equipment with little or no supervision. My boss was very impressed and never hesitated to sing my praise. It was hard to stay unnoticed by colleagues and clients at the printing press.

One day, my boss had a guest who wanted to publish a magazine and was being given a tour of our facility. They got to my part of the press, and I explained how the machine I operated worked. He asked me different questions, and I answered. According to him, my answers were intelligent and articulate. As my boss went to his office to take a call, the man looked at me and asked what a smart and beautiful girl like me was doing in that place; that was how I met JACOB.

***

I slept in a small wooden building at the back of the printing press, which was like a mansion compared to sleeping in the streets. It was a Saturday morning, and I was about to go outside to buy a loaf of bread for breakfast. As I got to the gate, the security man handed me a letter. I was so excited because it was from Miss Theresa, the only person in the world who knew where I was and truly loved and never disappointed me. I hurried back to my room and opened the envelope. As I read the letter, it seemed like the words were fading, black dots moving around and blurring my vision. Miss Theresa informed me that Banta, my dearest friend, took her own life after enduring rape from her husband, to whom she was sold.

This must be a dream!

Oh my goodness! Not Banta too!

Why didn't I take her with me?

Why didn't I help my friend?

What kind of friend am I?

What kind of life is this? What if she was a boy?

I can't think…I can't write…I can't breathe.

It felt like someone just drove a 7-inch blade through my heart.

The pain. Too much pain. Excruciating.

Sunday morning came. I was sitting on my mat staring into space, lost, confused, angry, and sick to the stomach all at once; I hadn't left my room since I read the letter. I couldn't muster the strength to eat. The security man knocked on my door and told me someone wanted to see me. It must be from my boss, who else knew me or where I was. I came out looking horrible; I was hurting and hadn't taken a shower or combed my hair, but I didn't care.

What was Mr. Jacob doing here on a Sunday? He saw me and was concerned about my look. He begged me to get in his car so he could get me something to eat. Why should I? He was just another man like every other one I had encountered. From my experience, no man gave anything free, so I wasn't interested.

"Please, Mr. Jacob, I am not having a good day, so if it's not about work, can I go back inside?"

"Wait a minute," he pleaded, "you don't look very well, and I just want to make sure you are okay, I promise. Please let me take you out to get some good food, real food."

His voice had a very familiar calmness. The comfort it brought wasn't strange. The sincerity seemed genuine, but I only got that kind of feeling from another person's voice. I had only felt that from Miss Theresa. I paused and looked at him closely.

"I can't go out like this; if you can wait for me to change my clothes, I will feel more comfortable."

He looked at me, smiled, and nodded.

Mr. Jacob waited until I was ready, and then he drove me to a nice restaurant. Trust me, I was too tired to wonder or ask him why he was so concerned and interested in my well-being. He tried to start up conversations, but I didn't hear a word he said. All I could do was imagine Banta's buyer violating her over and over again. I wondered how she cried every night and begged him to stop. My experience with my former Madam's husband made it so real that it hurt me even more. In my village, it was an abomination for a girl to tell anyone her buyer raped her. Her mother would kill her even before the stigma begins and no man would ever come to repurchase her. Banta was not so bright, but she was determined and hardworking. I couldn't stop wondering how she felt the moment she decided to take her own life. When Banta's lifeless body was found, there was a note in her hand addressed to me; Miss Theresa added it to the letter she sent.

The note read:

"Teno, my dearest friend, I have taken my freedom; I am finally free."

Tears began to roll down my face as we sat in the restaurant. Jacob was worried and quickly took me back to my wood house. He didn't care about the condition of my accommodation. He sat on the mat and asked me to pour out my heart. I gave him the letter to read then started my story from the beginning. By the time I was done, he was speechless. After a few minutes of silence, he told me that he came by to ask if I would be interested in working with him in his new publishing business. He was very encouraged to hear that I really wanted to be a journalist. The salary would be five times what I was getting at the printing press, and I would have a lovely apartment in his company's guesthouse. At that point, I didn't care about much anymore. I was just determined to succeed and make something of my life. I took the job.

Sitting in my own office as a community editor was hard to take in, especially considering I did not have a proper formal education yet. Obviously, my freedom was not too far anymore. I was working twice as hard and learning as much as my brain could handle. I vowed to learn all about success and everything that made the world go round. I didn't want to end up like my other friends in the village. I was enjoying my work, and I really appreciated the respect I got from my colleagues. They all came to me for advice and criticism. Hmmm...who would have thought that this girl from Kaminwanaga would be the one to provide solutions and help the city people in an office?

The fondness between Jacob and I grew so fast. For the first time, I had deep and true feelings for a man. I loved it. It came as no surprise when he asked me to marry him. He treated me like a queen, and I felt heaven on earth. I experienced a different kind of relationship between a man and a woman, which was so incredible. No one ever told me that a man could really love a woman and treat her like royalty. No one told me that a man had to ask a woman to marry him, and it would be her choice to say yes or no.

Was this real?

Is this how it is supposed to be?

Jacob bought me nice things I never imagined I could have, like expensive jewelry, shoes, purses, and perfume bottles. He gave me items I saw only in the magazines.

He would open the car door for me, let me choose what I wanted to eat, and tell me how much he loved me every day. I wrote to Miss Theresa, and in my letter, I gushed over this wonderful man who had changed my life and told her that he wanted to spend the rest of his life with me.

Miss Theresa replied like a mother, begging me to be careful and slow things down to learn more about him. What was there to find out beyond what I already knew? Her response to my letter hit me in the wrong place. I was infuriated when she inquired if I had sought God's face or spoken to my spiritual father about it.

Which spiritual father? In which church?

After my last experience in that church, did she really expect me to go to another church?

To seek whose face?

Where was God when my life was a mess?

Did I not pray?

Did I not fast?

Did I not keep my body holy until it was defiled?

Why did God not prevent that?

Do you know how painful it is to know that I cannot enter my marital bed as a virgin?

Don't worry; I could never speak to Miss Theresa like that. It was all in my head, but this was precisely how I felt.

Jacob was treating me well. The thought of him brought light and life into my heart.

CHAPTER SEVEN

Happily Never After

MY WEDDING DAY CAME, and it was beyond anything I could ever imagine. I can't begin to explain how amazing it felt. There were guests, friends from work, Jacob's family, lots of food and drinks. We even got gifts of all shapes and sizes wrapped in colorful wrapping paper. It was magical. It was beautiful. Jacob respected me so much that I didn't have to live with him till the wedding night when I moved in. I did not know what to expect that night as I had never had mutual sex, and no one told me what to expect on the day.

He went to take a shower and asked me to do the same.

I got to the bathroom and saw a fancy box that looked like an extraordinary soap dish. I tried to open it in a hurry so that I could finish bathing quickly. I didn't want to waste my husband's time. As I opened it with force, its white powdery content poured out and spilled all over the bathroom floor. I wasn't sure what it was, so I ran out to tell my husband about the accident. He hurried into the bathroom, and I saw this look of horror on his face as he stared at the content on the floor. He looked at me with bloodshot eyes and landed a very violent, stinging slap on my face that sent me crashing to the floor.

He warned me never to touch his 'COKE' again

Coke?

How?

On my wedding night?

Fresh out of my wedding dress.

There I was on the bathroom floor, on my wedding night, sore in the face, with tears in my eyes, and running make-up. "This cannot be happening," I thought to myself.

The next day, he begged continuously, insisting it was anxiety from the wedding and he would never do it again. I believed him because the Jacob I had grown to know, and love would never have done that. I forgave him and was committed to being the best wife in the world.

That was the beginning of the end. The beatings got worse, and the verbal abuse was more prominent than the word hello. I know that in Kaminwanaga, it was the norm for men to beat their wives because they owned them. Miss Theresa told me, however, that it was not usual for men to do that in the city. She said the police would make him stop. However, the city I lived in was not the "America" that she came from, so that did not work.

Jacob ordered me to stop going to work because he didn't want people to notice my bruises. This was so convenient for him because I had no family to run to. Should I leave and go back to the streets, or should I try to endure and do better so he could have a change of heart and love me again? I decided to put in more effort, which even made things worse.

He hit me at the slightest opportunity. When he was frustrated from work or when I watched television, he hit me. When I tried to look nice or ask him how his day went, he hit me. Even when I woke up, he would just hit me. When he started to beat me, he acted like an animal and didn't stop until he was tired. I wish I could explain what came over him when he got in that mood, but I cannot.

I got pregnant and lost the baby because he didn't stop beating me. It happened again with my second pregnancy, and this sent me to the emergency room. I was walking on eggshells in my own home. Was this not worse than being in my village? Then the cheating started, and the drugs took over. He was making phone calls in the middle of the night to various women and having very raunchy conversations with them, but I dared not ask any questions. While doing his laundry, I would find notes from different women in his pockets or receipts of feminine items he obviously did not buy for me. I dared not confront him. Jacob became a monster at home, but he was a wonderful man of the people and a philanthropist to the world.

Oh, God! Where is my freedom?

My life became a mess, and there was nothing I could do about it. Some might ask,

"Why didn't you go to the police?"

Believe me when I say that I did, but the result was worse. When the police came to the house to meet him, he took them into his study, and they were in there for about 30 minutes. They eventually emerged, and the two police officers were laughing and thanking Jacob. They referred to him as "Bossman."

What just happened?

Why are they walking away without warning or even arresting him? They saw my bruises, so why are they not doing anything? They left without looking back to say a word to me, and that was when I knew it was fruitless to involve the police.

Jacob walked them to their car, and when he returned to the house, he was mad that I had the nerve to go to the police. After beating me, he ordered me to move into the guest room and remain there. He reminded me that I was picked up from the gutters, where I belonged, so I did not have the right to share a room with him anymore.

I started staying in the guest room, but no one knew any of this was going on. We would go to work occasionally and play our roles as the perfect couple. In fact, we should get the awards for Best Acting in Real Life: Male and Female Category. The fact that I was relegated to the guest room did not stop him from coming in to get his daily dose of sex. He would come in drunk and smelly, with his own puke all over his clothes. He would not even bother to change or shower before climbing on top of me. There was no foreplay or anything of the sort; he just required absolute surrender and total submission on my part.

After a while, I got used to it and became numb as sex meant nothing to me. The experience I had the first time I was raped was the same one I had on my wedding night, and all through my marriage, nothing really changed. Before Jacob made me stop working, I would hear the ladies in the office talking about how much they enjoyed sex and even how they asked for it and complained when they didn't get it. My case was different. I always just wanted the sex to end immediately it started. All I had known about sex was pain and humiliation.

***

I got pregnant the third time and was so scared because I could not afford to lose this one. So, I did what Jacob wanted, how he wanted it. He would ask me to do unthinkable things to him for pleasure, and I would obey, just to avoid the beating. I had to protect my unborn child so, I became his slave.

One day, when Jacob was out with God knows who, I went to a hospital to register for antenatal care. As I went in to have my vitals taken, there was a class for pregnant women like me. I got curious and asked the nurse what the class was about. What she said was strange to me; she said it was organized by the doctor's younger sister for pregnant women in abusive relationships.

Wow!

I thought it only happened to people like me and not city women. The nurse started suspiciously looking at me and asked if I wanted a flyer with more information. I quickly replied with an emphatic "NO!"

When I was done with the doctor, I started walking towards my car when someone suddenly called out,

"Hello, Madam." I turned around, and the doctor's sister walked up to me. She introduced herself as JACKIE and told me about her class, which also served as a mentoring and counseling platform. She started doing this because she was also a victim of domestic abuse while she was pregnant. She lost four pregnancies and was told that she could not have kids anymore due to severe damage from the abuse. This scared the life out of me, and at that point, I knew I could not pretend anymore. I needed help and support to protect my child and survive the constant abuse, so I took her card and promised to call her.

After a few days, I called her and booked an appointment to see her during my lunch break. We eventually met, and I told her my story from my birth until that point. She felt so sorry for me and promised to help me. Jackie asked me several questions about Jacob, his business, his routine, his staff, those I could trust, and his drug and alcohol use. I gave her all the information which she wrote down in her notepad. When she was done, she looked at me and said, "This is what we have to do…".

CHAPTER EIGHT

No Time For Tears

MY ALARM WENT OFF, but I was so tired that I reached for my phone and put it on snooze. After a while, it rang out again. When I finally looked at the phone, I knew there would be trouble for me. You see, Jacob did not want any maid in the house. I did all I could to persuade and convince him, but he kept saying he wanted us to have the house to ourselves until we started having kids. The kids we could not have; because I kept losing pregnancies due to his constant beatings.

I jumped out of bed and ran to the kitchen to make breakfast. When I was done, I knocked on the master bedroom door where he slept and called out his name. Normally, he would respond because he usually woke up early and remained in bed for a few minutes. I called out his name again and asked him to shower and then come out for breakfast. He still didn't respond with his usual, "Stop disturbing me." My curiosity was greater than the fear of being beaten. It got the better of me, so I opened the door and realized he was not there; I checked the bathroom, and he was not there either. This was strange because I knew his routine. If he was not lying down, he was probably doing cocaine in the bathroom.

I hurried to my room and grabbed my phone to call the office, but he was not there. I called everyone we knew, his friends, partners, colleagues, and everyone I could remember. No one knew where he was, and I was starting to get very worried.

What is going on? Where can he be?

I called the police, but they told me to wait 24 hours before filing a missing person's report. I could not function because I didn't know what was going on or where he could be.

At about 4 p.m., the doorbell rang, and I was relieved, strangely, because I thought he had returned. When I opened the door, I saw two police officers who asked if I was Jacob's wife. Why were they asking me that question? Jacob's body was found in a hotel room. He had died from a drug overdose. They wanted me to come and formally identify his body; the young lady he spent the night with was already in custody.

Oh my! I didn't know whether to mourn him and cry

because I would miss him or whether I should rejoice and thank the universe for taking this burden off me. Trust me, these thoughts I am sharing with you are very private. If I had ever expressed these feelings at that time to anyone, the story would have been that I killed my husband to be free.

I went to identify his body but did not expect to be genuinely overwhelmed with emotions. Regardless of what he had done to me, he was still my husband. I could not believe he was the same person on the slab. He was just lying there helpless, lifeless.

It was so surreal; it felt like a dream. Could this really be happening?

Was someone playing a prank?

Was he going to spring up from the cold slab and tell me it was an elaborate prank?

Am I really a widow now?

Just a few hours after the news of Jacob's death had spread, people started trooping to the house from all over the city and nearby villages. They were all claiming to be members of his family. I recognized some of them from the wedding party; the others could have been aliens because I had absolutely no recollection of them whatsoever. He never told me about or introduced any of them to me. Jacob sold the 'orphan' and 'only child' story to me, and I bought it with all my savings.

Ah, Miss Theresa, I should have listened to you.

I was not alone; thankfully, Jackie was right there with two other women she was counseling. We had all become sisters who stood by one another through thick and thin.

Jackie came to me and whispered in my ear the most powerful words I had ever heard.

She said, "Teno, as you weep for Jacob, I need you to be very observant and vigilant. This is the time for you to be strong and wise. Identify those who are on your side and those who will use this opportunity to destroy you. These people here will start making their demands, but you have to go into your room and bring the package before they start. I will remove it from this house and keep it in a place where no one else but you will have access to it."

I wiped my tears immediately and ran to the room; Jackie followed me. When I brought out the brown envelope with the documents, she grabbed it and put it under the big black boubou (big flowing gown) that she wore. Her dress code was intentional because she had done it for so many other women in similar situations. She gave me a big hug and told me to start crying again as I walked out of the room. So, I started crying, and she acted like she was comforting me as we walked back to the living room.

You may think that we were heartless and dubious, but that is as far from the truth as the East is from the West. We knew what was at stake and what was coming; I was pregnant and knew my child would need all the care she could get. Did I mention that I was expecting a baby girl?

I still loved Jacob regardless, but I had to be intelligent and wise, like Jackie said. I had heard stories about too many women thrown into abject poverty as soon as their husbands died. They had lost everything to warring family members who contributed absolutely nothing to the business or estate of the deceased. So we put up a show for the so-called family members.

One of the elderly women walked up to me and said,

"Woman, we have come to discuss two things with you. The first is his property and how it will be shared; the second is your preparation for observing the widowhood rites according to our tradition."

An older man who claimed to be Jacob's half-brother said they had decided that I could have the smaller car I was already using. They would take the house and everything in it. They would also take the company and sell it to use the proceeds for his funeral. The elderly Woman, who first spoke, started listing the barbaric and insane things I had to do as part of the traditional widowhood rites. When she was done, I smiled and stood up. After greeting them with respect, I told them that I would decline any participation in the insane things they wanted me to do because I was pregnant. Nothing would make me lose this baby, and I did not care what anyone had to say about it. I made it clear that I was not interested in any form of rites or practice so they could leave my house.

As expected, they didn't take it very well. They jumped out of their seats angrily and came at me. Jackie and the two other women who came with her immediately stood in front of me. Standing between the hostile, supposed in-laws, Jackie told them to back off if they did not want to be arrested. At that point, Jackie picked her phone, dialed a fake number, and started talking to a fictitious police officer about harassment and attempted murder. The villagers stepped back and said they expected me to be out of the house before returning the next day. They also said they would leave two women behind to ensure I didn't remove anything from my home apart from my own clothes. I was not allowed to touch the cutlery, books, documents, or anything that belonged to Jacob.

I agreed and told them to give me time to pack my things. The villagers left angrily, leaving behind two of their representatives. Jackie, who already had the package, hugged me, confirmed I was okay to be by myself, and left with the two women. The village women followed me everywhere to ensure that I didn't take anything I was not supposed to take. I packed my things and left my home the following day.

***

Let me back up a little and explain the mystery behind the package and why I didn't fight back when these village people asked me to leave with nothing. Remember when I went to see Jackie for the first time, and she said, "This is what we have to do..."? Well, she told me exactly how to protect myself and secure a better future for my unborn child if anything ever went wrong. Please understand me; she was not hoping or preparing for him to die, but she had seen this happen countless times and knew it never ended well for the women. Jackie knew that I would be a statistic without the flawless execution of a well-thought-out plan. One who would get the short end of the stick in such situations; she did not want that to happen to me.

We started by drawing up a list of his properties, bank accounts, assets, and anything that could be turned into money. After that, we monitored his routine and discovered who knew about his assets. Jacob was a very paranoid and private person who didn't want his staff to know his worth.

Despite the turbulence that marked our union, I knew everything, as did his personal assistant; the only other person who knew was his lawyer. Jackie already gave me the strategy I needed to become very close to the assistant and lawyer without being sexual. I had to make them understand that we were all at the risk of losing everything we had worked for because of Jacob's secret addiction.

So, it was in their best interest to work with me to secure all his assets and make sure that they would both have a percentage of everything regardless of the outcome. They had to understand that at the rate Jacob was going, he could destroy or even sell the company to keep up with his habit, and we would all lose. So we had an agreement, added my name to the properties and company documents. We also added my name as a signatory to most of the other accounts. I promised to give them their share and had to sign a contract to the effect. It was agreed that no matter what happened, they would still keep their jobs and receive their monthly paychecks in addition to getting their percentages.

The next assignment was to get Jacob to sign over everything to me without his knowledge. It was not hard to achieve because I knew his routine, especially when he was very high. All I had to do was wait until halfway through injecting himself, then go quickly to him to sign documents. At those moments, he was always very impatient and cranky; he wanted to get everything over and done with so that he could return to his thing. As planned, I took the documents prepared by his lawyer and personal assistant to him at the right time and simply watched as he hurriedly grabbed and signed them. He asked me to make sure I gave him a detailed report on what he had just signed the next day.

The following day, I sent him the most detailed report I had ever written. I even made sure to say that his lawyer, accountant, and assistant were aware of the contract. The agreed story was that we had awarded a contract to a China-based company to replace our printers with better and faster machines. This supposed replacement was to help us beat our competitors, as our company had to be the best. We made this report so believable that he did not even argue. He just asked if the accountant signed off on it and could afford it without being affected so much. The personal assistant had already done his job convincing the accountant who just wanted to have a job and a constant flow of income. When the accountant came to see Jacob, he assured him that this was the best move and we would make our profit in less than a year.

Mission accomplished! We had done what we planned, and it was successful. As far as I was concerned, we didn't do anything wrong; we just wanted to secure our futures. If Jacob's drug addiction had not threatened the livelihood of his staff, if he was not cheating on me, and killing my babies, maybe things would have turned out differently. If he had not refused help from his assistant and lawyer, we most likely would not have needed to do all we did.

Unfortunately, he died from his own overdose in a hotel room with another woman. Yes, I am sad that my husband died, but forgive me for being honest. I am glad we took steps to protect ourselves. Now you know why I didn't even argue or fight when his so-called family members asked me to leave the house we lived in. That house was the smallest property Jacob had; the other properties and assets were unknown to his family, let alone talked about. Their ignorance about what Jacob was worth worked in my favor. Even the company they thought they could sell was already mine, so they could not touch it. Now you know what the package is all about. I was asked to leave with nothing, but they didn't realize that I had already moved everything that I really needed to another property. I was a widow, but I was a different kind of widow; I was a smart and fast widow.

CHAPTER NINE

Up and Away

THE COMPANIES WERE STILL RUNNING with the same staff, and everyone was happy about that. I made sure that everything ran smoothly. I also made the personal assistant, Mark, the new Managing Director because business was good.

At this time, my pregnancy was already advanced, and I had some complications. Jackie advised me to have the baby in the United States of America, where they would take better care of my baby and me.

I applied for an American visa and went for the interview. They asked me so many questions, which I answered to the best of my knowledge. I showed them all the documents in my name to show that I was not running away because I had assets here. Then I told them about my pregnancy complications with supporting documents from the doctor and the American hospital I had communicated with.

I was denied the visa, and all I was told was, "I am sorry, Ma'am, you do not qualify for the visa."

I was very disappointed.

Why would they not let me go to the hospital in their country when I would spend my own money?

Miss Theresa called my home phone just to find out how I was doing with the pregnancy. She also gave me an update about Kaminwanaga, "We now have one phone center in the village owned by a man who came from the city."

That was great news because I didn't have to wait for weeks to get my message across to her. She also said that this same man set up three film viewing centers where the villagers could pay some money and sit in the small room with only seven people. There was a little television on the wooden table with a machine that could play the film. The only issue he faced was that the village elders had to see the movie and approve it before people could pay to watch it. They didn't want anyone to bring Western ideologies or make the girls start to think they could be something other than what they are. I bet it was also a way for these old men to see Western movies free of charge.

I really missed home so much. I was not happy about the issues there, but I really did miss my home. Miss Theresa paused and asked, "What is wrong, Teno?"

Although I tried to act as if everything was fine, she had a way of making me tell the truth.

"I've developed some complications with the pregnancy. I tried to get a visa so I could get treatment and have the baby safely in the U.S., but I got denied the visa."

My heart was broken, and she felt so sorry about what I was going through. She was also confused and did not understand why the embassy would deny me the visa knowing my medical condition. I told her that I thought her American people would be as nice as she was because the person who interviewed me was rude. She said she was not surprised but asked why I said they were her people.

Are they not her people? After all, she came from America as a missionary to help the young girls from Kaminwanaga.

She laughed so hard.

"Teno, I am from Canada, but I lived in America for a few years to do some missionary work which eventually brought me to your village. I am Canadian and not American, and I am almost certain this must have come up in one of our conversations here in Kaminwanaga."

Wait a minute. How was I supposed to know the difference at the time? As long as you were white, with long hair, you were from America. However, if she had mentioned it when she first came, I am sure everyone in class missed it. We could barely understand a word of what she was saying then.

She asked me, "Why don't you go to Canada? They have amazing hospitals there, and the Canadians are very nice and warm people. Try to apply again with the same proof and supporting documents; let's see how it will work out. I'll make a few calls and see what additional documentation I can help you with."

I took her advice and went to the Canadian embassy. They didn't even ask me any further questions when I told them about my complication. They gave me the visa, and shortly after, I left for Canada.

***

Wow! Abroad.

My goodness, is this place real? Why is everyone

so friendly to me? So this is where Miss Theresa comes from? Why in heaven's name did she agree to go to my village? Why would you give all this up to suffer with us in KAMINWANAGA? Why did she love us so much? If I stopped believing that there was a God up there, it was my mistake. I had more than enough proof that God was real.

The trip was my first time on a plane, and I must admit, I was a bit scared, but the white lady who sat next to me noticed my plight and spoke to me so kindly. The stories of her naughty but loving grandkids, 80-year-old husband, and travels around the world captivated me. Listening to her got my mind off being bundled together with people in this big metal tube with wings, just cruising over the open ocean. We had to trust the pilot to have his eyes on the sky at all times.

Two days after I arrived, I finally checked into the hospital to have my baby. Then I became popular amongst the nurses and doctors. They were fascinated with my accent and just wanted me to keep talking. Gradually, I started telling them my story and the journey from my village to the city, my life with Jacob, and how I got there.

They found my story intriguing and my resilience inspiring. Each time the doctors and nurses came in with all their gadgets, neat lab coats, and overalls, they always wore a smile. They were either always just happy to see me or genuinely satisfied with their jobs. I felt very safe in their care.

Finally, my baby girl arrived!

She was so beautiful and strong. The fact that she came naturally surprised me because of the complications I developed back home. Oh my goodness! She was so beautiful; I could not even contain myself. I had never seen a baby this beautiful and calm. I named her Banta.

Yes, I named her after my dear friend. The other mothers, nurses, doctors, and people I didn't know would come by my room just to say hello. I was not used to that, but apparently, it was customary for strangers to say hello to new mothers.

I was playing with my daughter when a woman walked into my room with so many things for the baby. She brought water, milk, diapers, wipes, baby clothes, and other things. I told her she probably came to the wrong room because I didn't order any of those things. She laughed and said it was their policy and that I would receive all this free for another six months.

What?

Free?

How?

Why?

I was in total shock.

After a few days at the hospital, the doctor came in and said he wanted me to stay in Canada for a few months so that he could observe my daughter and me. It was standard protocol considering my complications during pregnancy.

With the help of the hospital and a few people I met during my stay, I got a small apartment for us to stay in temporarily. Before I was discharged, I notified the hospital I would pay cash for my entire bill before leaving, and I was surprised they gave me a 50% discount! Wait a minute! Who does that? Somebody up there in the sky must really have been looking out for me.

The two-bedroom apartment was small but very

comfortable; it had everything I needed. There was constant power, and I must say it took me a while to get used to that. I kept ironing my clothes the night before if I had anywhere to go the next day. I was so paranoid the lights would be out in the morning. I didn't want to show up with wrinkled clothes. You can laugh at me, but I am sure every immigrant from my country to the Western World can relate. There was central heat and cooling. A washer and drier in the apartment. Everything worked just fine. I quickly realized that you didn't have to be super rich abroad to have the basic necessities like constant power, clean water, and access to good transportation.

Life in Canada was comfortable and calm. Some people might say it was because I had a lot of money to do whatever I wanted, which is fine; I earned it. I went into the doctor's office for check-ups four times a month and was not asked to pay a dime for any of them. In the wee hours of the morning, I would call my office back home because of the time difference, just to get updates, check on the accounts, do follow-ups, and send emails when I had to.

One day, I went grocery shopping with Banta. While I

was standing in line, waiting to pay for the things I bought, I observed a little girl, about ten years old, standing in the same line in front of us with her mother and older brother. The brother couldn't have been more than a couple of years older than her. While she was busy helping her mother get the items out of the shopping cart and placing them beside the cashier's register, her brother stood by the magazine stand. He kept staring at the magazine covers with beautiful models. The little girl noticed her distracted brother and called out, almost irritated, but respectfully,

"James, do you mind giving us a hand here, please?"

James didn't hear a word. He picked up one magazine and flipped a page. Their mother was caught up with the pile of groceries in front of her. She was clearly used to the brother versus sister episodes and wasn't going to be a part of it this time. I observed keenly from a few feet away. Confidently, this young girl walked to her brother, who was admiring the models in the magazine.

"James, you do know that this is not how these women really look, right? Most of them have cellulite, stretch marks, and spots. These pictures have been photoshopped to make them look flawless and perfect. An entire generation has been deceived into believing this is what a perfect body should look like. They are causing girls to starve themselves sick to achieve this representation of a perfect body that is close to impossible to maintain. So, instead of helping the women in your life, here you are, a fully immature young man, just drooling over images that are not real. I bet this will become your standard for the ideal woman you want to date or get married to; what a shame."

She shook her head and rejoined her mother, who by then was searching her wallet for either cash or her credit card to pay the cashier. James sighed, placed the magazine back on the stand, and rejoined his family.

What? Did I just witness that? Did that ten-year-old kid just school her older brother? How did she become that confident? How could she use such words at that age?

Wow! I looked at my daughter Banta and knew the kind of life I wanted for her. There was no doubt in my mind that she had to be in an environment where she could be bold, confident, articulate, and free to express herself. This is her right. She deserves it.

After thinking long and hard about our next steps, I got a lawyer and told her everything. I asked what my options were; we went with the student visa option for staying in Canada.

Apart from the training we got in the village from Miss Theresa, I never attended a real school. Other than what she taught me, which was enough to survive in the city, I had nothing.

The lawyer assured me that if we informed the Canadian immigration of my situation, my willingness to go to school and invest some money in a company that will employ Canadians, they would let me stay.

We went through the process, and they granted us a residential visa that would let us stay there for two years, after which we would have to renew.

I registered a publishing company, got my daughter into a program, and started attending school.

When the two years were finally up, I decided to renew my visa. This time, they gave me a permanent resident card because the company was doing well and my grades were excellent. I could not go to college because I had not been to a formal grade school, let alone high school. So, I attended a professional business and entrepreneurship training school for two years to get a certificate, not a degree.

My daughter started developing into an amazing, intelligent and beautiful girl who had the kind of education and exposure I dreamt of as a little village girl. She attended one of the best public schools in Winnipeg, so we didn't have to pay any school or bus fees; breakfast and lunch were also complimentary.

I had been in Canada for a few years, but I still could not get over the free things we were getting.

After a while, a prestigious Canadian university sent me an email asking me to speak on child marriage issues and how it affects Africa.

Despite my nervousness about this, I gave the talk. The event facilitators were so pleased that they introduced me to the school president; this meeting led to other speaking engagements.

Surprisingly, people started paying me to speak about

issues affecting women in Africa. To think that my misfortunes and painful experiences in life had turned into profit for me.

I watched my daughter grow and benefit so much from the Western world. She was allowed to speak her mind and learn about technology and sports.

WOW!

Why can't we have the same thing back home?

Why can't we have schools where young girls can learn to read and write?

Why can't we raise our daughters to know who they are and explore their talents?

Why can't the young girls of my village have even a fraction of what my daughter has right now?

I called the phone center in my village and asked the man to tell Miss Theresa to give me a call as soon as she could.

In the meantime, I started reaching out to all the people I had met while I was in school, the universities, and other companies that had hired me to speak. I told them that I needed them to support me in the project I was about to take on; it was a project that could not be handled by one person alone.

The next day Miss Theresa called me and what I shared with her made her cry over the phone. She didn't cry out of pain or anger; she was shedding tears of joy. We both knew that this mission would be dangerous and we would face a lot of resistance, so I had to come prepared. She knew I needed all the help I could get. So, as promised, Miss Theresa reached out to her first church in Canada, the church in America, some of her relatives, and people who she knew would love to be a part of this.

My daughter Banta was about ten years old and was already done with elementary school. I decided to have the conversation with her because I felt she was old enough to understand everything I wanted to tell her. She had so many questions to ask about my village and the way the young girls were treated. Banta also wanted to know about her grandparents and uncle, so I answered her questions. What Miss Theresa did for me excited her.

When I told her about my plans, she was happy and supportive. She asked if she could come with me. Hmm! I was not sure if I was ready for her to experience that kind of environment.

After thinking about it for a few days, I felt it was vital for her to know where she came from. She had to learn about their practices, how fortunate she was to be born and raised in a place where her rights were respected.

We packed our things in excitement and flew back to Africa.

CHAPTER TEN

Back To My Roots

I FIRST GOT TO THE CITY so that I could tidy up a few things in my company. A few years after I left, Mark, the personal assistant who ran the company in my absence, had to leave the headquarters. I needed him to help stabilize one of the smaller local branches that almost went bankrupt. Our creative director had to take over the day-to-day running of the company and did a great job.

I walked into the office with Banta, and the staff started screaming in excitement. I did not tell anyone that I was coming except Jackie, who was kind enough to pick us up from the airport. We spent a week in the city doing some things in the office. I was brought up to speed by Jackie on the plans. I had asked her to be on the board of my project, and she was so helpful.

The time came to go to Kaminwanaga. I almost had cold feet because I had not been back or spoken to any member of my family since the day I got on the bus and left. Jackie was my source of support and promised to be by me every step of the way.

When we got to Kaminwanaga, my daughter was very fascinated with everything she saw. She asked questions and kept pointing at every animal, every hut, every woman who tied a wrapper on her chest, and every man tapping palm wine on the tree.

Our first stop was Miss Theresa's house. When we parked in front of the house, she came out. I broke down and cried my eyes out as we were in a tight embrace. I didn't want to let go because I had missed her so much.

Miss Theresa looked much older but was still very beautiful and strong. In fact, she looked like she was very comfortable and blended more with the people. I looked at her again and shook my head. Still wondering why she stayed for over a decade with all the oppositions, threats, and challenges she faced because she decided to help young girls in the village.

She knew me well enough to know what I was thinking and what she said to me blew my mind:

"When God sent me to this village, I didn't understand

why. The day I met you, I thought it was because I had to help you somehow. So, when you left the village I thought that my work here was done. However, the Holy Spirit kept asking me to stay back because my purpose here had not been fulfilled. It took over ten years to finally realize what that purpose was, and it was still connected to you. The day you told me about the project, the Holy Spirit told me it was time to fulfill that purpose. This project is what my being here was all about. So, thank you for letting God use you."

Wow! This would be a revolution, and I was just so honored to be a part of all this. She grabbed Banta and gave her the tightest hug of her life. Before I knew it, they were both talking about Canada and speaking with their Canadian accent. Trust my Banta to talk about landmarks, school, her friends, and everything she could remember.

I introduced Jackie to Miss Theresa since they only spoke to plan and execute the project over the phone. We spent the night at Miss Theresa's house and talked for hours that night. I had never seen Miss Theresa that animated and excited. I knew she was thrilled to see me again and excited to see Banta, but it was so different.

We went to my father's house the following day. When we got there, I saw a guy sweeping the compound. As soon as he heard our car arrive, he looked up. I came out of the car and smiled at him, not knowing what kind of reaction to expect. It was my brother Mebo; he looked spent and much older even though he was younger than I was. He looked like life was being sucked out of him, and it made me feel bad. Let me back up a bit and tell you why I was feeling bad.

When I started doing well in the city, I did all I could and sent money and gifts several times through Miss Theresa. They were all returned with a message from my father saying, "We don't need your money or gifts. I knew that my father said way more than Miss Theresa said to me. He must have said unthinkable things to Miss Theresa, but knowing her, repeating his words was something she would never do.

After a while, I stopped trying because I knew how stubborn my father was. My mother, Denka, could not accept all I sent behind his back because if she were caught, she would've been punished for it.

Now you can imagine how I felt seeing my brother in that condition. For some reason, he didn't recognize me. I panicked. I called out his name and told him it was me, his big sister, Teno. He screamed, gave me a tight hug, and would not let go. He started crying and asking me to forgive him. I didn't know why he asked me for forgiveness, so I started crying and asked him to forgive me too. As that was going on, a woman came out asking Mebo why he was yelling. She came out, and when she saw me, she recognized me immediately and started screaming her lungs out. As she cried, she said, "MY DAUGHTER IS BACK!!! SHE HAS COME BACK TO ME, THANK YOU, GOD!"

As we hugged and cried, my daughter Banta came to me and asked if the woman was her grandma and if the man was her uncle; when I said yes, my mother grabbed her in a tight embrace and cried some more.

My brother was still looking like something was off. I asked why he didn't recognize me immediately. That was when he said he started losing his sight a few months before then. They didn't know what was wrong even after going to all the local healers in the village. It was too painful for me to hear. I didn't want to discuss it around the house.

My mother invited all of us into the house and thanked Miss Theresa for all she had done. I also used the opportunity to tell her all about Jackie, who was still taking everything in.

When we were done with pleasantries, I asked about my father, Beba. The whole place went silent. I asked again, and Mebo said, "Papa died a few weeks ago, and according to his wishes, we buried him quickly and quietly. He was very ill. His body started changing and smelling. A few days to the day he died, he didn't want anyone to visit him at all, and he said his burial should not attract people. He didn't want them to see his remains like that."

My father passed away, and I didn't have the opportunity to make up with him. I didn't introduce him to his granddaughter. I did not get to say goodbye.

The Revolution Has Begun

MISS THERESA HAD ALREADY HIRED the right people to start working on the project. It was as if God provided everything I needed to make this come true. She got grants from several organizations in America and Canada to help kick off the project. One of the American organizations sent a representative to oversee the finances and make sure things were going according to plan.

Mebo and I were in our father's house alone to really talk about his eyes and see what could be done to help. I sat with him in the living room. As we started talking, he told me how our father died with too many regrets. His biggest regret was treating me the way he did and not giving me a chance to be who I wanted to be. He was too stubborn to admit it or say it to anyone, but they all knew. Mebo told me that he became sad and withdrawn. No one could get through to him, but they all knew how much he missed me.

Whenever Miss Theresa came with a message from

me, he would turn her away, then go inside his room and cry.

I didn't understand it. If he loved me and missed me that much, why didn't he just let me see him or talk to him? I guess I will never know.

Mebo's eyes were getting worse, so I sent him to the city to get proper treatment.

Banta wanted a tour of my village. Jackie wanted to come too, so I asked Miss Theresa to go with us as she knew more about the developments than I did. We set out and started walking through the market and the village square. Memories came flooding into my head, but I did not know how to feel anymore. They were unpleasant memories, which I wished could disappear. My consolation was that my daughter did not have to grow up with such memories.

As we walked through some houses, I saw someone watching us but didn't know who. After a while, I stopped and followed the person. I asked the person to please turn around so I could see her face because I knew she was following us. As she turned around, I recognized her. It was Tando's mother. She was much older and worn out, looking so unhappy and lost.

I hugged her and asked how she was doing; she looked into my eyes and said, "I wish I knew better, my dear. I miss Tando so much, and I know it was my fault. I was not even allowed to get her body and bury her."

It broke my heart to see her like that. She was no longer herself, spoke very incoherently, and was sad. At a point, she entered her own world, and I knew she had developed some psychological issues.

The news of Tando's death did not come as a shock to me at all. Don't forget that I saw her in an abandoned forest with other girls when I went there with Miss Theresa and Miss Mary. I wish there was something I could have done to save those girls from all that horror. It was painful for me because I didn't know much then. I was too young to do anything about it.

According to tradition, once a girl was taken there, no one could get her out. Even when they died, their families could not touch their bodies as they were considered contaminated and evil. The village council elders would ask some young men to go and identify the dead girls and throw them in a pit dug behind the building.

I didn't know what Tando and the girls suffered from at the time, but now I know it's called VVF (Vesico Vaginal Fistula).

Why? This could have been avoided. The men responsible for this did not, and still do not, understand the dangers their actions pose. To them, the solution to the problem was, and remains, sending the girls to live in the forest until they die.

***

If I ever doubted the saying that the apple does not fall far from the tree, Banta erased all my doubts. Sometimes, her inquisitive nature gets to me, and for an African mother, it gets too much. Miss Theresa, on the other hand, being a teacher, sees it as an excellent developmental process. So, during our tour, she asked lots of questions which Miss Theresa clearly loved to answer.

She wanted to know everything about the women carrying wood on their heads, the men on the trees getting the palm wine drink, the kids playing in the river, and many other things. I cracked up when she told me how much she wanted to play with the kids but decided to wave from afar when she saw how big the river was.

After a month of planning, preparation, meetings, and training, it was time to meet with the elders at the Village Council. I had to talk to them about my project; it was, as the Bible says, a Time for War.

CHAPTER TWELVE

Time To Act

MISS THERESA CALLED US OUT to the living room to pray before the meeting. Though her prayer was long and very emotional, for some reason, she sounded a bit scared of what was about to happen and tried to hide it. After getting ready, we set out for the meeting. We got there to meet the arena already full.

We wondered why the men, who were sitting down waiting for us to arrive, had come earlier than the agreed time. As the custom dictated, there were no females in the arena apart from Banta, Miss Mary, and me.

Regardless of age, women were not allowed to be present at meetings, let alone become members of the Council of Elders. The men usually met to make the decisions, and the women had no choice but to abide by them.

Being considered foreigners, Miss Theresa and Jackie were not allowed into the arena, so they sat on the bench outside, waiting.

I started my speech by greeting the elders and the men present, and then I went on to talk to them about the project.

My first mission was to explain and educate them on the rights of women and young girls based on what I had learned from the developed world. I tried to make them see why child marriage and depriving the girls of a proper education were destroying their lives. They needed to know the benefits of educating girls and allowing them to contribute to the village's growth. After saying all that, I then told them about my project.

A tuition-free All-Girls School in Kaminwanaga, where girls learn to read and write in English, know basic calculations, science, social studies, history, and art. All I needed was their blessing to proceed. I had already bought the land, finalized the building plan, and commissioned the builders.

When I was done, their spokesperson, who happened to be the man who wanted to marry me as a child, stood up to speak. He started yelling at me without deliberation and told me that I was a disgrace to the village. He asked me who my daughter's father was because he was sure I didn't even know. Then he made it clear that they would never allow anyone to come into the village to change their traditions and culture. He also said I had no right to bring the white man's way of life to destroy their daughters' minds.

The next question he asked me got me angry, but I controlled my anger because my daughter was already scared. He asked me if I had circumcised my daughter, and emphatically I said, "No, and it will never happen to my child because I know better."

The whole arena almost went up in flames as the men started yelling. I immediately asked Miss Mary to take Banta outside because it was getting out of hand. I wanted her to have an opportunity to speak to the elders and tell them what she had been learning. I wanted them to see the benefits of educating young girls, but things quickly went south.

As she was taken outside, I was ready to face these men without fear because I was not about to back down. I didn't come all the way from Canada to be scared off by these old men.

I kept quiet until they were done yelling. Then I told them that everything would go on as planned, but it was their choice if they didn't want their daughters to come to the school. However, as far as the law was concerned, I had bought the land.

Let me back up a little bit, in my village, women are not allowed to buy or even own land. So Miss Theresa called Bishop William, the missionary who had visited my village before I was born, and sent her to Kaminwanaga. She told him about my plan and explained the issues with acquiring property. He agreed to help us buy the land using his name.

To the villagers, Bishop William owned the land. There were legal documents between the Bishop and me to show a change of ownership since I bought it from him. They started arguing and said that the land belonged to the Bishop, so they would not let me use it for the school.

The school would be a dream come true for both of us because I wanted a change in my home. Though Miss Theresa did her best to teach the girls in her house, much could not be done.

The spokesperson, who had taken his seat after his tirade, stood up and told me that we had to leave the village and return to where we came from if we didn't want trouble. We had one week to do as we had been instructed. Then he started threatening me.

At that point, I could not explain what came over me; now that I think of it, Miss Theresa's prayers seemed to have received answers at the right moment because I was not afraid. In fact, I looked straight at him and told him that I was a true and proud daughter of Kaminwanaga. I had not committed any crime, so he had no right to send me out of my village.

At first, he didn't know what to say, and then he looked at the other elders hoping to get a response from them to back up his threat.

I told him that according to the land laws, my daughter and I had not done anything punishable by banishment. It was also against our tradition to send innocent, law-abiding foreigners away from the village. I thanked them for their time when I was done talking and stormed out of the arena, leaving them to argue amongst themselves.

After the meeting, we all went to my father's house to see my mother. I told her what had happened at the arena and how upset and disappointed I was. She laughed and asked me what I was expecting; how I thought I could change the tradition with one meeting.

Of course, I knew it would be difficult, but I didn't think they would be aggressive and mean.

When she asked what I planned to do next because she was scared for my safety and well-being, I had nothing to say because I was too angry.

Miss Theresa started praying again and asking the Holy Spirit to give us wisdom. Still, I was too angry to join her because the Holy Spirit should have been there to make them listen to me as far as I was concerned.

Miss Mary suggested that we ask Bishop William to speak to them, but my mother said it would worsen the situation. He was a foreigner who would be seen as coming to disrupt their way of life.

With everyone lost in their own thoughts, the sound of silence in the living room was deafening. After what seemed like twenty minutes, Banta, my daughter, spoke and said,

"Excuse me, mummy, if those old men won't listen to you, why can't the women and the girls talk to them by themselves? My teacher always said that we should never be afraid to ask for something if we wanted something. If we are determined not to take no for an answer, we must keep trying and never give up."

That was it!!! Banta had just given us a brilliant idea. That was the only way it could work.

I told my mother what the plan was, and she screamed, "Do you want them to kill us?" I told her that nobody could kill her. My people may be opposed to change, and civilization but they are not murderers. They just want to do things the way they have always done and continue to live in their ignorance. Their practices are harmful and may often result in death, but nobody will kill you for demanding change.

We spent hours talking and convincing her until she finally agreed. She saw that this was worth fighting for, and if it would make her a scapegoat, so be it.

The next phase was to visit the women. Those who

had lost their daughters to harmful traditional practices like female genital mutilation, VVF, domestic violence, suicide, and many other issues.

We also visited women who went through these things and were still stuck in a life where they felt helpless. We spoke to them and tried to convince them that they needed to speak up for the generation of girls who still had the chance to make a difference.

It took us almost five days to go round as many houses in the village as we could because it had to be at the time when their husbands were out of the house. We had to do a lot of work and planning, but with my mother and Miss Mary's help, we could get to at least 90 percent of the village's female population.

By the time we were done, we had noticed that every woman and girl had gone through horrible things from the day they were born; no one was spared. It was shocking to see some women I grew up thinking were happy in their homes talking about being forced into marriage. They could barely communicate in English, let alone write. So, it was essential to fight for this change and save the lives of these girls.

Good News! We were able to convince almost all the women and their daughters.

It was time to Act!

CHAPTER THIRTEEN

Change Has Come

SEVEN DAYS AFTER THE SHOWDOWN with the Council of Elders (the day we were to leave the village), all the women and young girls gathered in front of the market. They were ready and determined to change their narrative. I stood there in front with my daughter Banta, my mother, Miss Mary, Miss Theresa, and Jackie. It felt so unreal because I had neither witnessed nor heard of such a thing in my village. We were about to make history.

The women of KAMINWANAGA have never been able to fight for anything or even have a voice to speak up for themselves. However, they were ready on this day, and nothing could stop them from getting their desired results.

Jackie had pulled some strings in the city to get media houses into my village to cover this peaceful rally. I didn't know that she teamed up with Miss Theresa. She got the American media to broadcast live feeds from the city media.

When the press arrived, my mother explained to the

other women that this rally would be witnessed by the whole world.

Oh my goodness! You will not believe the excitement it caused. Even those who could not speak proper English were willing to go in front of the camera to tell the world why they were out to speak up today.

My mother led the rally and started chanting things that the women would respond to or repeat. Something like, "ENOUGH IS ENOUGH"; "LET OUR DAUGHTERS LEARN"; "STOP CHILD MARRIAGE" and "STOP CUTTING GIRLS," All in our native language.

Word spread around the village about the rally, and people started coming out to see this unbelievable thing happening. They were more intrigued by the media and the cars that were in convoy.

Some men who heard that their wives were a part of the rally came to try to disrupt it. They ordered their wives to go back home or face the consequences but were shocked to see their wives continue chanting and walking.

When the men started threatening their wives, my

mother walked up to them and told them that the press was there to show the world how they treated women. She warned them to back away so that the world would not turn against them.

These men (who were also not educated) believed it when we told them that America would send an army to deal with them if they hurt anyone. They humbly complied and walked away, which made us laugh so hard. It was our day, the day when women would finally be heard, and nothing was going to stop this from happening.

We finally got to the village square. This time, we all walked boldly into the arena, which was usually not acceptable. There were too many of us. Some women had to stand outside. The Council of Elders were inside the arena when we walked in, but the other men were barred from entering.

It was interesting to see some women telling their husbands that they could not enter until we were done with what we came to do. Of course, we maintained the story of the whole world watching them.

This time, I knew it was not my place to speak. My

mother spoke first. I was so proud of her that a tear dropped from my eye. That was when I knew that she never really liked or supported what my father did but had no choice. The other women and young girls took turns to speak their minds and demanded that they be allowed to learn and decide whom to marry. They also told the elders that they could work and earn enough to take care of their parents when they learn in school; instead of being sold off in marriage because of money.

As the women spoke, the press recorded and took notes as well.

When we were done, one of the city pressmen asked the elders what their response was and how they intended to handle the issue. The elders were not prepared for this. Because they were not so fluent in English, they decided not to embarrass themselves. They then asked one man who could speak proper English to respond on their behalf. To my greatest shock, this man was Tando's father.

As he spoke, his voice trembled, and he almost broke down. He told the press about his beautiful daughter and how his belief and traditional practices deceived him into forcing his little girl into marriage. This resulted in the disease killing her. He also spoke of how his wife suffered from a mental illness because she could not get over Tando's death.

At the end of his speech, he told the press that he would personally support the school by volunteering to help with the construction of the building.

The women and the press gave him the loudest applause I had ever heard; I was so inspired and happy.

It all felt like a dream, one from which I didn't want to wake up. The elders could not say anything at that point; they just nodded their heads and said okay.

WE WON!

We were so happy that we danced and sang all around the village. Miss Theresa thought it would be good to lead the women to the land on which the school would be built.

As we got there, they all prayed over the land and hoped it would provide the change they were longing for and save the girls' lives born into Kaminwanaga. I turned to my mother and gave her a tight hug. Banta, who did not like to be left out, joined in too.

The building construction commenced, and we were shocked at the number of volunteers from the village who wanted to make sure the school was built quickly. After three weeks, Banta, Jackie, and I went back to the city.

I saw my brother, who was already undergoing treatment. He was looking much better. The companies were also doing very well, which made me so happy.

It was time to go back to Canada so that Banta could resume school.

***

10 months passed, and the school was finally ready. Philanthropists, churches, non-governmental organizations, and individuals who saw the rally on the news had sent in all the supplies we needed from America. Miss Theresa and Miss Mary were there to receive and place them where they were meant to be.

Banta was now on holiday, so it was time to go back to Kaminwanaga to witness the opening of the building. We got to the city and spent a few days so that I could have the opportunity to oversee the books and accounts in the company.

Jackie also had to get herself ready for the trip.

The trip was smooth and quick.

When we got there, we went straight to Miss Theresa's house. I was so anxious I could not wait to see the school. Banta and I begged Miss Theresa to let us go and see the building, but she refused because she didn't want to spoil the surprise.

That night I was unable to sleep. I couldn't believe that I was about to make history for my people.

The day finally came when we would declare the school open and start operations. We wanted the staff to get used to the system and the documents before even admitting students. Everyone needed to agree on the style of uniform and other materials that the girls would need. Miss Theresa asked me what the school's name should be, as we had not named it. That was not my priority at the time; I just wanted to set the ball rolling.

On our way to the school, we stopped by my father's house to pick up my mother. She looked prettier than ever. I held back the tears because I don't remember ever seeing her all dressed up with her hair beautifully done. As a married woman, she was not allowed to dress up and look that nice so that other men would not stare at her. If they did, it would be her fault, and her husband would punish her.

After about an hour, it was time to head to the school, and we were all so excited. We eventually got to the building gate and parked the car because I wanted to walk in and see how everything looked.

When we walked in, I fell on my knees and cried. It was more beautiful and colorful than anything in my village. Banta came to me and asked me to stop crying. The staff employed by Miss Theresa and Miss Mary started walking to me to say, "Welcome, Ma." The villagers all came in turns to hug me and say, "Thank you." My mother grabbed my arm and told me how proud she was of me and how she wished my father was alive to see this day. She then asked about my brother; I told her he would be on his way to the village to join us for the opening.

When I got inside the building, I walked through the classrooms, library, offices, restrooms, cafeteria, sickbay, chapel, and staff quarters with everyone else walking behind me.

It was too overwhelming; I could barely speak. This experience was everything I dreamt of and even more.

The staff took us to the auditorium where the main event was taking place. People were sitting and waiting already.

The press was there again; they were so happy to see how the school turned out, so I thanked them for being a part of our history and sharing our story with the world.

When I eventually got up to the stage to speak, I saw Tando's parents and Banta's father. That was when the name finally came to me, and I said,

"I will name this school after my good friends Banta, which is also my daughter's name, and Tando. The name is Bando All-Girls School (BAGS)." Everyone loved the name. They all became very emotional.

We left the auditorium and walked to the academic building to cut the tape off the door and officially open the school. The atmosphere was filled with joy and laughter. The women started singing and dancing. I looked at Miss Theresa and Jackie and started crying because I had never met women who were so loving and supportive. I could never have done this whole thing without them. I asked where Miss Mary was and learned she was called away to receive a message from the village phone center on behalf of Miss Theresa.

As the celebration continued, my mother was at her best entertaining guests and thanking people for coming. She looked so radiant. I immediately knew that she would do a great job as the Matron of the school.

Suddenly, I saw Miss Mary walking towards us, but she looked sad and uncertain. I asked her what was wrong, but she avoided my eyes, smiled, and said she wanted to talk to Miss Theresa and me privately. We walked into the nearest room, the library, and sat down to hear what Miss Mary had to say.

Miss Mary went away to receive the call from one of my staff members who called from the hospital; my dear brother Mebo had passed away that morning.

As they were treating Mebo's eyes, they discovered that his heart was damaged and deteriorated over the years. He asked them not to tell me or anyone else. He was an adult who had a right to ask for doctor-patient confidentiality.

I could not believe the wrong turn the day had taken.

Mebo did not live to see this day, just like my dad.

What do I tell my mother?

How do I tell my mother?

How do I break the news on a day like this?

Why is this happening?

I am tired of losing people!

Miss Theresa walked out to bring my mother into the library. I hugged her so tight and told her about Mebo. She cried but held it together because she didn't want to ruin the event.

Wow! I did not expect this because I had seen him a few days before, and he looked healthy.

We all agreed to name the library after him "THE MEBO LIBRARY."

We buried Mebo next to my father.

My mother was at least comforted by the fact that she had the schoolwork to keep her busy, and Miss Mary promised to spend time with her on weekends.

Let's just say God blessed me with angels who would be there for me through thick and thin.

Miss Theresa would become the Principal of the first

all-girls school in my village, and Miss Mary would serve as Vice-Principal.

To my greatest surprise, Bishop Williams and some organizations in Canada sent missionaries to come and train the staff and help with documenting, registering, exams and certificates, etc.

BAGS was adopted by Miss Theresa's church, which promised to send books, materials, and everything that would help the school grow and develop.

I caught myself shaking my head and saying, this is too good to be true. Miss Theresa heard me and said it was by the power and grace of God who made it all possible.

Finally, our girls can go to school. They can be who they want to be. They can choose their husbands when they are ready. From now on, the phrase, "Màmá, it's a girl," will no longer be a source of sorrow and anger. People will rejoice when they have daughters.

A change had come to Kaminwanaga.

◀◀◀◉───EPILOGUE───◉▶▶▶

If a young girl from a remote village like Kaminwanaga can make a difference and bring change to her people, so can you.

You don't have to build a school to make a difference.

It could be donating books, computers, teaching a skill, donating sanitary towels, providing water, giving out blankets, providing shoes or sandals, etc...

Whatever you think you can do to help others, please do it.

Every girl deserves an education.
Every girl deserves to make her own choices.
Every girl has a right to live.
Every girl deserves love and respect.
Every girl has a right to say no.

#MamaItsAGirl!

◄◄◄—DEDICATION—◊►►►

This book is dedicated to all the women and girls whose rights have
been violated.

Those who have been deprived of their essential needs because of
their gender.

Those who don't have a voice and are treated as second-class
citizens.

Those who have been persecuted because they dared to challenge
the norm.

Those who are executed because they refuse to bow to harmful
practices.

I stand with you all! This is your voice!

Your truth will be heard.

#MamaItsAGirl!

◄◄◄──SPOKEN WORD──►►►

They taught us to smile through the pain.
My goodness, that's insane.

They said, regardless, silence is golden.
But then my virtue was stolen.

You are an AFRICAN woman, don't speak.
I am shattered. I am in pain, and it has reached its peak.

You are a girl; this is what we all go through.
I am human first, and this is not my truth.

Education is wasted on girls; what's the point?
You never know how it can change the world, so let it be my
choice.

You have to marry him, leave school, it's your father's wish.
I want to fall in love, learn more, tour the world and check off my
bucket list.

He is a man, so he will earn more.
I am a woman; what if I do more?

It's a man's world, it's his house, you are just a tenant.
You got it all wrong; it's our world; I am the lieutenant.

◀◀◀━ NOTE FROM THE AUTHOR ━▶▶▶

Thank you for reading this book. I cannot tell you how grateful I am that you have decided to support the women and girls of the developing world just by reading. If we all come together and spread the word about how their rights are being violated, the world will listen because there is strength in numbers.

It is loosely based on real-life events, told through one person (an African girl). In reading this story, the goal is to entertain and sensitize the reader regarding the issues raised.

I was honestly afraid of writing this because not only is this my first book, I didn't want to start with a sensitive and emotional story. It was scary to imagine what or how readers would feel. It took 6 years to get the boldness I needed to set the ball rolling.
The millions of women and young girls who needed people to hear them were my biggest motivation. Their very existence made me decide to take the plunge and contribute in my own little way.

Thank you for being a part of this journey; I truly appreciate it.

A percentage from the sales of this book will go to some of these victims in Africa who need books, sanitary towels, education, skills acquisition, etc.

Please don't keep this to yourself. Spread the word and encourage others to get this book.

If this has impacted you and you would like to chat, please send an email to info@stelladamasus.com; I would love to hear from you.

Thank you,
Stella Damasus

◀◀◀ ——— DEAR READER ——— ▶▶▶

*Thank you again for purchasing this book. I am very grateful
to you for supporting my work and the STELLA DAMASUS ARTS
FOUNDATION.*

Just a reminder to:
*Please leave a review on Amazon or any social media platform you
wish to share it on*
Let others know I am available for interviews to discuss the book.
Share the Amazon link to your contacts
Buy it as a gift to loved ones and friends
Suggest it as your next read for your book club
*Recommend #MIAGBook on social media for your followers to
know about it and get their own copy.*

*A percentage of the sales goes to the STELLA DAMASUS ARTS
FOUNDATION, where we support and partner with other non-profits
that care for women, young girls, children's education, food, shelter,
and medical treatment.*

www.sdartsfoundation.com

Printed in Great Britain
by Amazon